FANTASTIC 4

THE MOVIE STORYBOOK

TWENTIETH CENTURY FOX PRESENTS IN ASSOCIATION WITH MARVEL ENTERPRISES, INC. A 1492/BERND EICHINGER PRODUCTION IN ASSOCIATION WITH CONSTANTIN FILM "FANTASTIC FOUR" IOAN GRUFFUDD JESSICA ALBA CHRIS EVANS MICHAEL CHIKLIS JULIAN McMAHON KERRY WASHINGTON MUSIC BY JOHN OTTMAN MUSIC SUPERVISOR DAVE JORDAN FILM EDITOR WILLIAM HOY, A.C.E. PRODUCTION DESIGNER BILL BOES DIRECTOR OF PHOTOGRAPHY OLIVER WOOD EXECUTIVE PRODUCERS STAN LEE KEVIN FEIGE PRODUCED BY CHRIS COLUMBUS BERND EICHINGER AVI ARAD RALPH WINTER WRITTEN BY MARK FROST AND SIMON KINBERG AND MIKE FRANCE DIRECTED BY TIM STORY

www.fantasticfourmovie.com

FANTASTIC 4

THE MOVIE STORYBOOK

Adapted by Catherine Hapka

Based on the motion picture written by

Mark Frost and Simon Kinberg

and Michael France

HarperKidsEntertainment
An Imprint of HarperCollinsPublishers

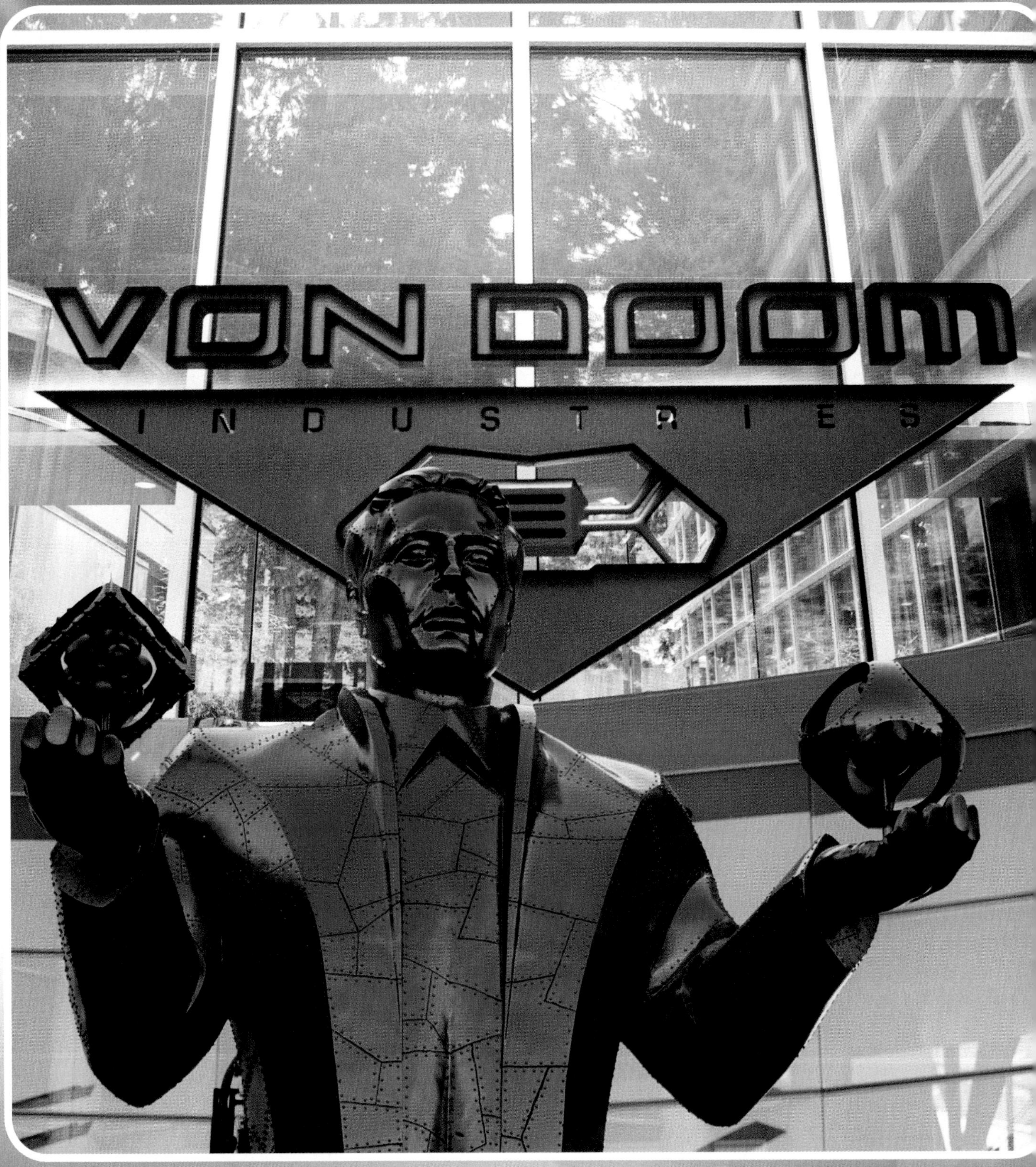
VON DOOM
INDUSTRIES

"Executive elevator, top floor."

Reed Richards silently followed the receptionist's directions. He and his friend Ben Grimm were paying a visit to Victor Von Doom, an old college classmate who was now a wealthy businessman.

"Why are you nervous?" Ben asked Reed in the elevator. "What's he got that you don't?"

"A billion dollars and his own space shuttle," Reed replied grimly.

Reed, a brilliant scientist, wanted to explore a distant cosmic storm to find cures for human diseases. But first, he needed a financial partner to help him get into outer space.

"Same old Reed," Victor drawled. "Always reaching for the stars."

"Back in school we talked about working together," Reed said. "That's what I was about to explain. . . ."

Sue Storm entered the room before Reed could finish his sentence. She was Victor's Director of Genetic Research—and Reed's ex-girlfriend.

"How have you been?" Reed asked her.

"Never better," Sue replied coolly.

Victor agreed to Reed's plan. As he told his Director of Communications, Leonard, the mission would be good publicity for the company.

Reed, Ben, and Sue talked over their flight plans.

"I was hoping Ben could pilot the mission," Reed said.

"He's welcome to ride shotgun," Sue replied. "But we already have a pilot. You remember my brother, Johnny, don't you?"

Johnny was a cocky young pilot who had once worked for Ben at NASA.

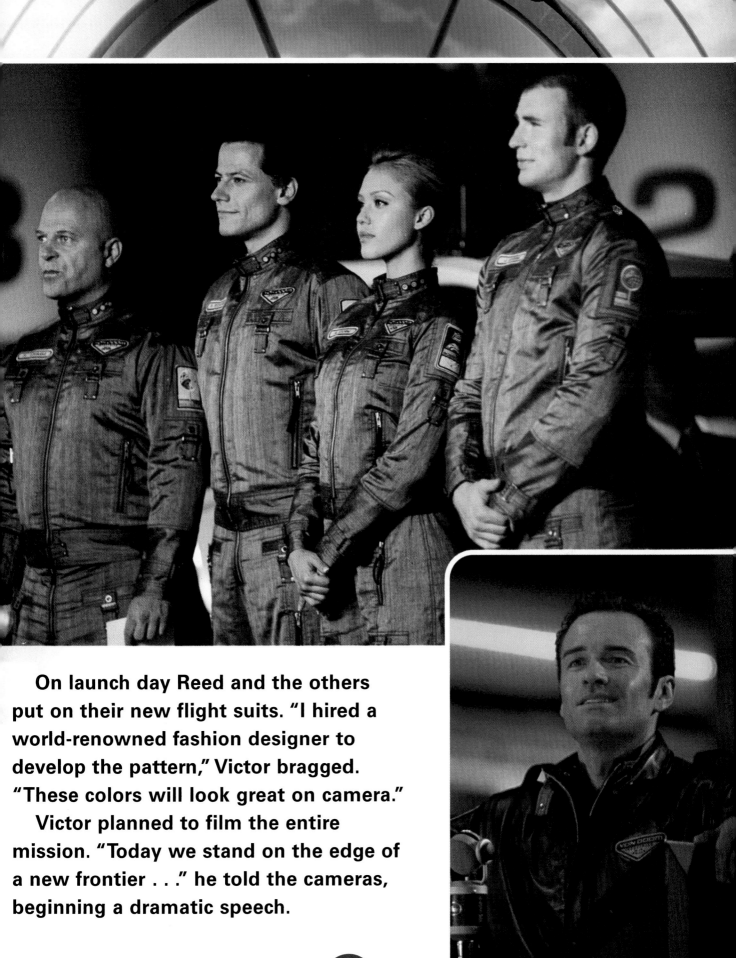

On launch day Reed and the others put on their new flight suits. "I hired a world-renowned fashion designer to develop the pattern," Victor bragged. "These colors will look great on camera."

Victor planned to film the entire mission. "Today we stand on the edge of a new frontier . . ." he told the cameras, beginning a dramatic speech.

Reed, Ben, Sue, and Johnny were almost ready to go. Ben's fiancée, Debbie, hugged him tightly.

"Get back soon, or I start looking for a new groom," she joked.

Boom!

The thrusters fired, and smoke billowed up from the launchpad. The shuttle lifted off, blasting through the atmosphere.

Soon it was safely docked at a space station orbiting the earth. Reed, Victor, Ben, Sue, and Johnny gathered in the station's command center. It offered a fantastic view of the earth far below.

"Long way from the projection booth at the planetarium, isn't it?" Sue said to Reed.

Reed was surprised by her friendliness—he thought she was still angry about their breakup. "Yes," he said. "Yes, it is."

Victor led Sue away to a different part of the station. He was planning to ask her to marry him, but before he could get the words out, he was interrupted by a shout from Reed.

"The cloud is accelerating!" Reed cried out in horror after checking his instruments. "We've got minutes until it hits, not hours. My numbers were wrong!"

Ben was already outside setting out the sample boxes for their experiment. Reed knew he had to get his friend back inside—fast!

Reed and Johnny rushed to the air lock to signal Ben. Ben turned and saw the cosmic storm rushing at him.

Inside, an automated voice announced, *"Event threshold in two minutes."*

Victor radioed from the command center. "Reed, we're running out of time! Get up here so we can close the shields!"

But Reed wouldn't leave until Ben was safely inside, and neither would Johnny.

Victor started to raise the safety shields. That meant the others would be trapped outside them.

"You can't leave them there!" Sue cried.

"Watch me," Victor said grimly.

Sue rushed out. She had to help her friends!

Reed and Johnny watched Ben struggle to reach safety. Finally he grabbed the edge of the air lock door—just as the first particles of space dust pelted him.

"Event threshold in ten seconds."

Johnny hit a button to close the outer air lock door as Sue rounded the corner.

Then the storm hit and everything happened at once.

Control panels sparked and flamed. Vapor and smoke were everywhere. Space dust slipped through the outer doors as they slid shut.

Finally the cosmic storm passed. In the command center, Victor crawled out of the rubble. He was unhurt except for a few scrapes and a thin cut on his head.

Reed, Johnny, and Sue dragged the unconscious Ben out of the air lock.

"Ben, wake up!" Johnny cried.

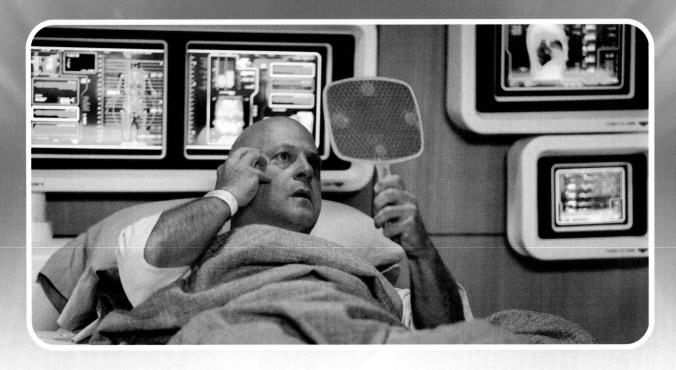

Ben didn't awaken until they were back on earth. Victor took them to his private hospital in the mountains.

All the crew members were supposed to be resting, but Johnny decided to sneak out and go snowboarding. As he shot down the mountain, something strange happened—his body started to smoke and flame!

Ben, Reed, and Sue sat in the dining hall. As Ben ate, his stomach grumbled loudly.

"Are you all right?" Reed asked.

"I think I need to lie down." As Ben walked away, he noticed that his stomach was actually *moving* beneath his shirt.

Left alone, Reed and Sue talked about their old romance. But the conversation soon turned sour.

She shook her head. "You're unbelievable, Reed. You never got it and never will."

Suddenly Reed noticed something very strange. Sue was *disappearing*!

"Sue, look down!" Reed cried.

Sue glanced down and saw her clothes floating in midair. As she screamed and jumped to her feet, she accidentally knocked a bottle off the table.

Reed grabbed for the bottle, even though it was too far away for him to catch. Suddenly his arm stretched two feet out of the end of his sleeve!

Johnny heard the commotion and rushed into the room. The three of them tried to figure out what was happening.

"It has to be the cloud," Sue said. "It's altered our DNA!"

"We have to find Ben!" Reed cried.

Elsewhere, Victor noticed some changes, too. The cut on his face had become an ugly scar, and instead of fading away the scar was growing!

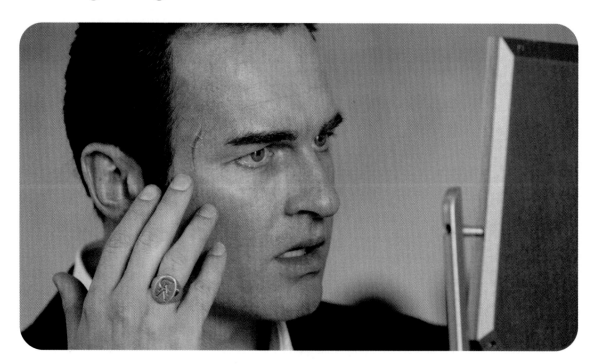

Ben refused to come out of his room, so Reed used his rubbery arm to reach under the door and unlock it. By that time Ben had escaped through the window. All the others saw was what looked like a huge creature running away.

Ben rushed home to New York City. He went to Debbie's house and called her outside.

"This is going to be a shock," he warned from the darkness. Debbie gasped as he stepped into view. He was twice his former size, and his skin was orange and lumpy.

"Don't touch me!" Debbie screamed.

Later Ben sat brooding atop the Brooklyn Bridge. He just wanted to be left alone. But he accidentally caused a big traffic pileup on the bridge.

Reed, Sue, and Johnny soon found him and could hardly believe their eyes.

Ben was surprised by the changes in his friends, too. But there wasn't time to talk about it. A fire truck coming to help with the accident swerved right through the guard rail!

Ben's monstrous strength was the only thing that could save the firefighters. He grabbed the truck and, inch by inch, dragged it back onto safe ground.

Everyone on the bridge cheered. Meanwhile, the others helped to control the damage with their new powers, too.

"We're scientists, not celebrities," Reed told a fireman a little while later.

"Try superheroes," the fireman replied. "They're calling you the Fantastic Four."

"Cool," Johnny said.

Reed made a statement to the press explaining what had happened to them on the space shuttle. He also explained that none of them understood their special powers yet.

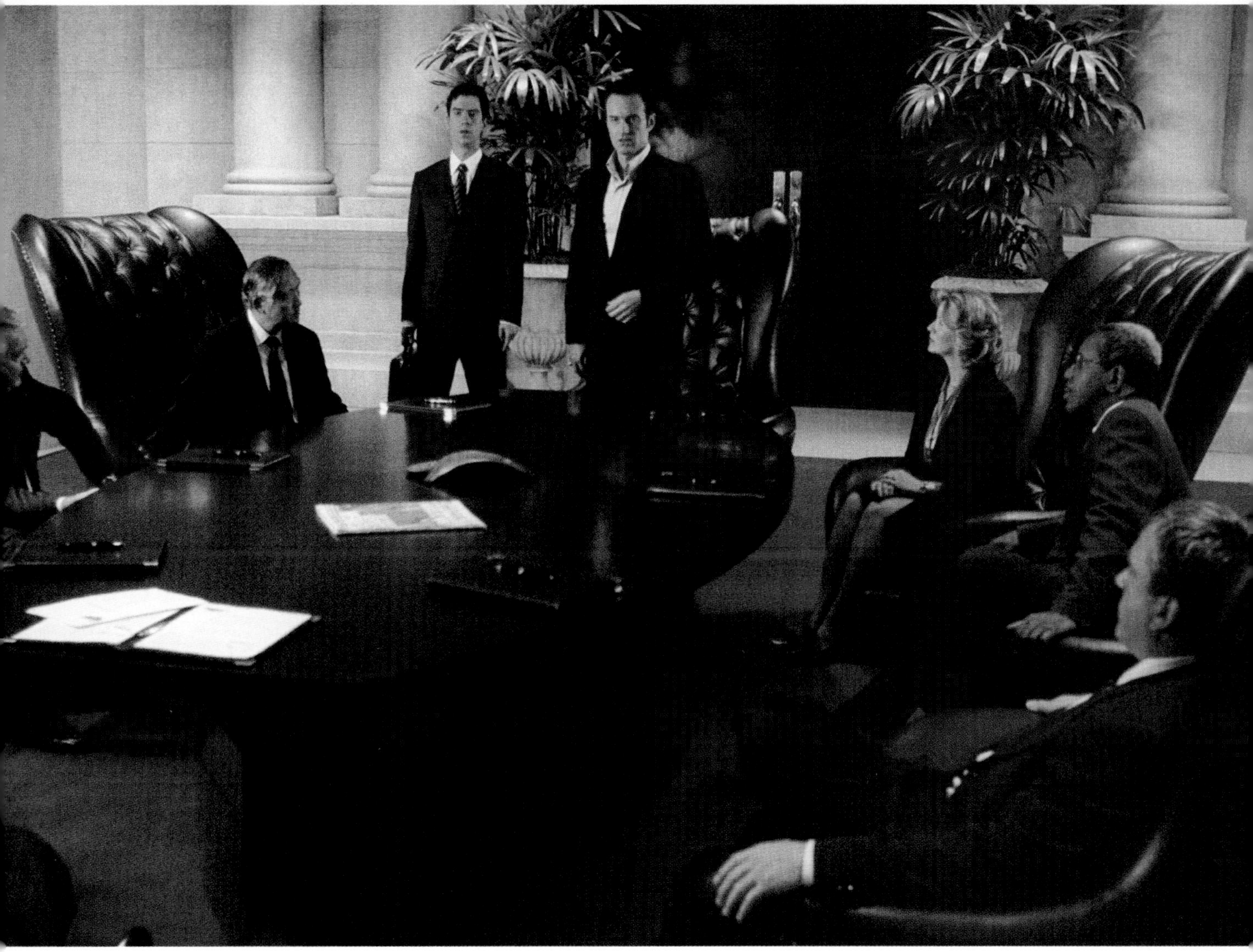

Victor and Leonard saw Reed's comments on TV. "Nobody wants to invest in a company that turns its workers into circus freaks," Leonard exclaimed angrily.

But Victor had a plan. "If I can cure these freaks, then I can cure anyone," he said. "What better way to restore our company's reputation?"

He had no time to spare—otherwise his company would be ruined. The bankers who helped to fund the business were already threatening to pull out.

The friends returned to Reed's offices in the Baxter Building. Reed wanted to figure out exactly what had happened to them.

"If I can understand it, then I can control it."

Reed experimented on his friends, learning more about their powers. He discovered that the uniforms they'd worn in space could stand up to their powers—Johnny's uniform could withstand the heat, and Sue's uniform disappeared with her—while normal clothes couldn't.

Victor was learning things, too. His body was changing into the same superstrong metallic substance that had formed the shields on the space station. He was also becoming extremely strong.

Reed tried desperately to figure out how to change his friends back to their normal selves. He studied the results of his experiments and scribbled formulas on chalkboards.

Feeling depressed by his new form, Ben went to a bar in his old neighborhood. All the patrons fled when he entered . . . except one: Her name was Alicia Masters, and she was blind.

"You look okay to me, mister," she joked.

Then she felt Ben's face with her hands. Even then she wasn't afraid.

"Sometimes being different isn't a bad thing," she told Ben.

Johnny wasn't depressed by his powers at all. He went to a motocross rally and showed off some of his new tricks, riding a motorbike through crazy jumps and spins. He even figured out that he could fly!

TV reporters at the rally wanted to know more about the Fantastic Four. "So what are your superhero names?" they asked eagerly.

"I go by the Human Torch," Johnny replied, making it up as he went along. "We call my sister the Invisible Woman."

Reed and the others watched on TV as Johnny told the reporter that Reed's new name was Mr. Fantastic, while Ben was known as the Thing.

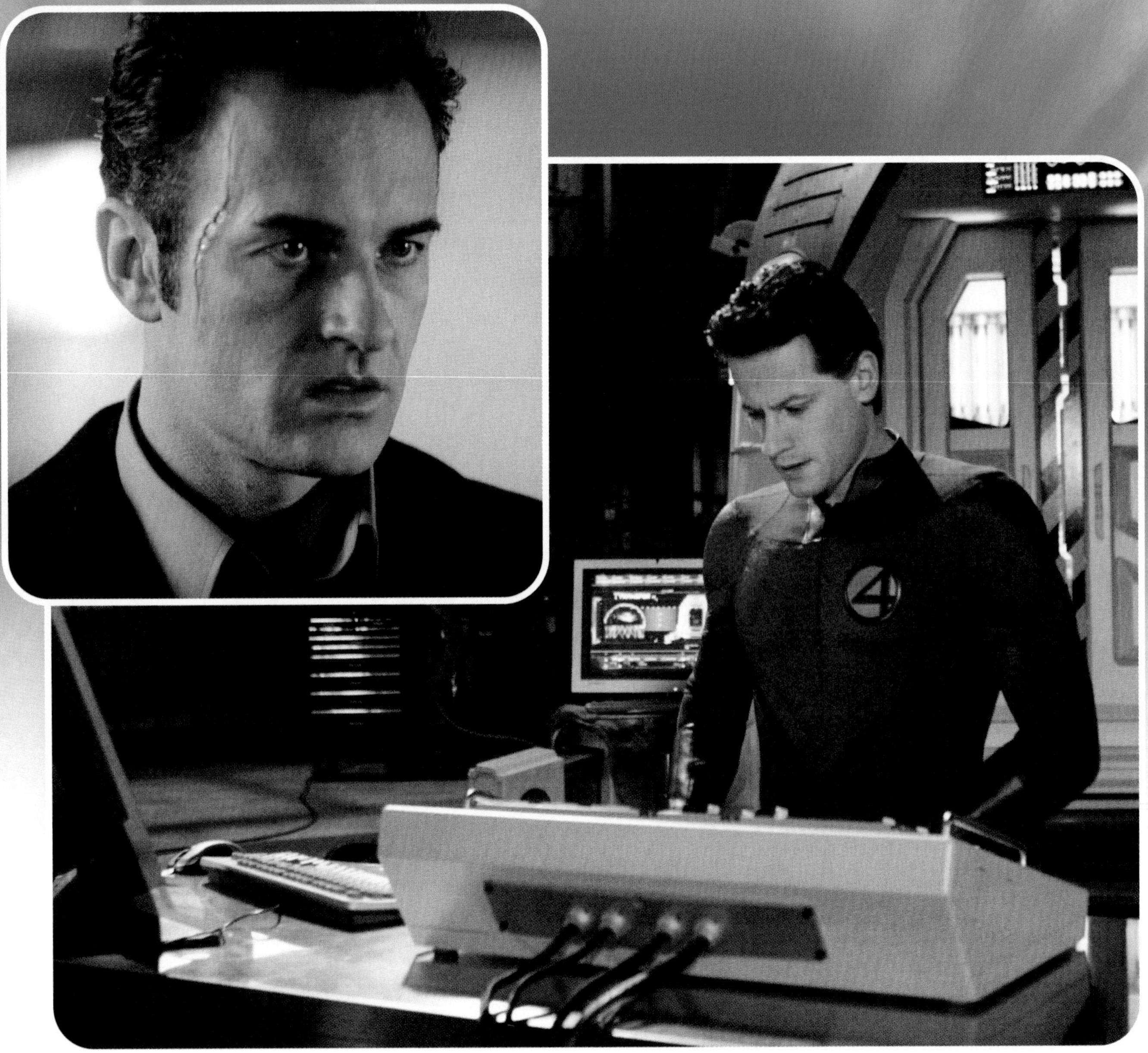

The others weren't impressed by Johnny's antics. But they had a bigger problem. Victor was pressuring Reed to find a cure.

Luckily Reed had a plan. He wanted to build a chamber with leftover shields from the shuttle, then create a particle storm to reverse the effects of the cosmic storm.

"How long till it's ready?" Victor asked.

"Three, four weeks," Reed replied. "I need to be sure the storm's stable."

Victor's workers built the chamber. But Reed still wasn't sure he was ready.

"Don't let Victor push you to get what he wants," Sue warned him.

But Victor was sneaky. He convinced Ben that Reed didn't care about curing him. That made Ben angry, and the two friends had a big fight.

Reed felt so guilty that he decided to test his cure right away—on himself. But the chamber didn't work. It didn't have enough power.

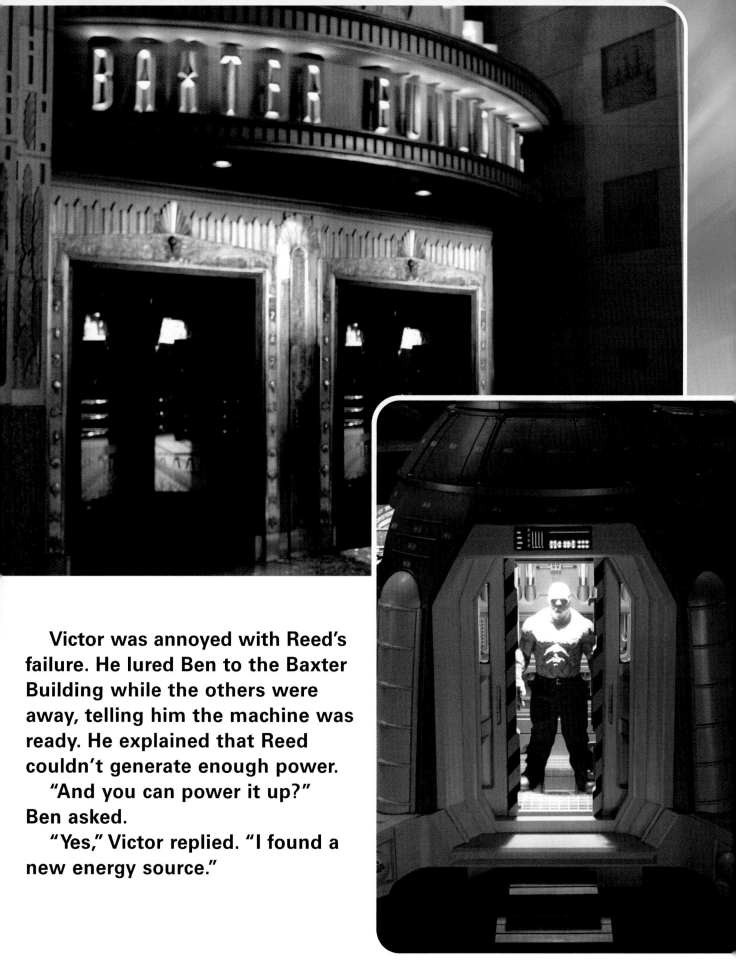

Victor was annoyed with Reed's failure. He lured Ben to the Baxter Building while the others were away, telling him the machine was ready. He explained that Reed couldn't generate enough power.

"And you can power it up?" Ben asked.

"Yes," Victor replied. "I found a new energy source."

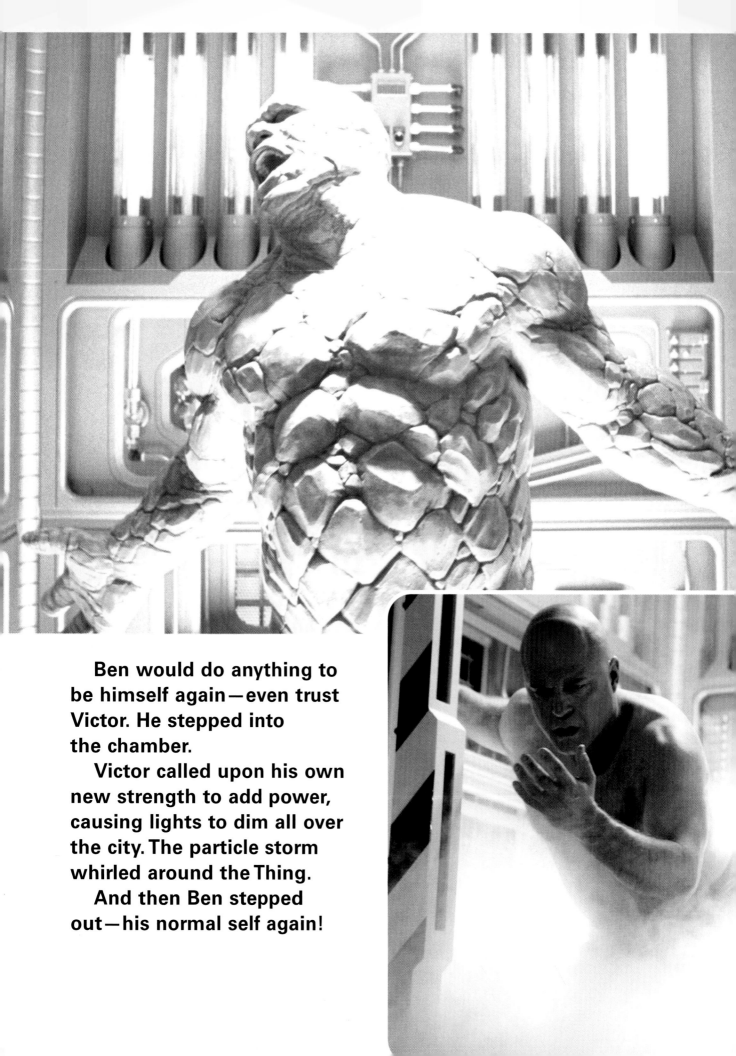

Ben would do anything to be himself again—even trust Victor. He stepped into the chamber.

Victor called upon his own new strength to add power, causing lights to dim all over the city. The particle storm whirled around the Thing.

And then Ben stepped out—his normal self again!

Ben's happiness lasted only a moment. He realized that Victor had been changed by the experiment, too. Now he was calling himself *Doctor Doom*!

"I've always wanted more power," Doom growled. "Now I've got an unlimited supply!"

He blasted Ben, sending him flying across the room.

"One down, three to go," he said, gloating.

Reed and Sue saw the lights flickering all over the city from Doom's power surge. They quickly figured out what was happening and raced to the Baxter Building.

But they were no match for Doctor Doom. He blasted Reed right out a window. Then he sent Sue crashing into a wall, leaving her buried in a pile of rubble.

Doom left the building, grabbing the limp Reed on his way out. A moment later Johnny arrived on the scene and found Sue.

Doom took Reed to his offices and left him in a freezing-cold room.

"Chemistry 101," he taunted. "What happens to rubber when it's super cooled?"

Reed could only watch helplessly as Doom fired a missile at the Baxter Building.

Johnny saw the missile coming. It zeroed in on him because of his body heat. He flew up and led it away from the building, finally guiding it straight into a garbage barge, where it exploded.

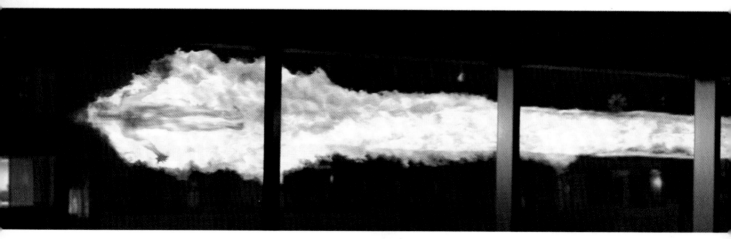

Meanwhile, Ben was realizing he couldn't help his friends. In his old body, he was too weak.

Sue recovered and soon found Doctor Doom and Reed back at Doctor Doom's offices. She tried to reason with Doom, pointing out that Reed could change him back.

But Doom wasn't interested. "Do you really think fate turned us into gods so we could refuse these gifts?"

Sue was left with only one choice. She attacked Doom—but he was too strong! Reed watched the whole scene with frustration. There was nothing he could do to help.

"I've been waiting a long time for this," Doom explained, gloating as he prepared to finish the two of them off. "It's my time now!"

"Wrong, Tin Man," Ben announced. He had turned himself back into the Thing! "It's clobberin' time."

Ben, Sue, and Reed battled against Doom, crashing out of the building in a furious struggle. Before long Johnny returned to help them.

The Fantastic Four fought Doctor Doom all through the city streets. Alone, each would have been no match for him. But by combining their powers, they vanquished him . . . by flash-freezing him into a huge metallic statue.

The crowd that had gathered to watch cheered wildly.
"I love this job," Johnny said.

Even Ben had to agree with him. He picked up the Doom
statue as Reed and Sue finally kissed.

As they all walked off together, Johnny shot off a few
fireworks. They were a team now . . . a family.